THE CHASM

RANDY ALCORN

THE CHASM

A JOURNEY TO THE EDGE OF LIFE

MULTNOMAH

THE CHASM

Trade Paperback ISBN 978-0-525-65335-6
Hardcover ISBN 978-1-60142-339-9
eBook ISBN 978-1-60142-340-5

Published in the United States by Multnomah, an imprint of the Crown Publishing Group, a division of Penguin Random House LLC, New York.

MULTNOMAH® and its mountain colophon are registered trademarks of Penguin Random House LLC.

The Library of Congress has cataloged the hardcover edition as follows:
Alcorn, Randy C.
    The chasm : a journey to the edge of life / Randy Alcorn.— 1st ed.
        p. cm.
    ISBN 978-1-60142-339-9—ISBN 978-1-60142-340-5 (electronic)
I. Title.
    PS3551.L292C47 2011
    813'.54—dc22
                                            2010036052

147468846

To
Nanci Noren Alcorn,
my very best friend,
with whom it is a distinct privilege
to walk the red road, in honor of our beloved Chasm-Crosser

I also want to give special recognition to Kristopher Orr, art director at Multnomah Books, and to Thomas Womack, Ken Petersen, Kathy Norquist, and Doreen Button for their comments on the manuscript. Finally, Mike Biegel deserves credit for his excellent artwork and his responsiveness to my ideas and input. Thanks and best wishes, Mike!

ONE

For most of a day, I'd been climbing a sharp incline of rocks and shale, toward an outcropped ledge that would afford a better view than anywhere else in this strange land. Finally, scrambling up the last twenty feet, I stepped out on that ledge and looked. What I saw took my breath away.

There it lay, stretched out against the horizon as far as I could see—the thing I'd been warned about, the thing I'd been told was ultimately unavoidable. The sight of it was even more devastating than I'd feared.

Here I was, hoping to travel to the distant shining city, a world of wonders I absolutely *had* to reach. For my first thirty years, I'd never dreamed such a place even existed. Then when I started to believe it might, I tried like the devil to avoid thinking about it, for reasons I still don't understand. And now here I stood, all hopes of reaching that magical place dashed. Before me lay the biggest obstacle imaginable.

No, it was absolutely *un*imaginable. That great yawning chasm sucked all hope from my heart. An abyss of staggering proportions. I had once stood with my family, when I had one, gazing down into the Grand Canyon. For a few minutes I'd been swept away by its grandeur before needing to pack up the kids, grab a hamburger, and get to the hotel. But this endless rift, this hole in the universe, made the Grand Canyon appear, in comparison, like the grave I dug when ten years old, to bury my old dog Ranger. It seemed infinitely large, deep and foreboding, containing not a shred of beauty. The chasm meant that the city calling to me from afar lay forever out of reach.

All that mattered for me was that place I could still glimpse on the horizon, far beyond the impassable barrier spread out below me. *I had to get there*—I had to reach that stunning capital of a great undiscovered country, that shining city that rested on the great white mountain. The place named *Charis*.

My name is Nick Seagrave. My story is true, though what world it happened in is hard for me to say. The memories burn in my brain, more real and weighty than what we call the real world. Before I tell you the incredible events that unfolded next, what happened to me at that chasm, I must first take you back to explain what led up to the moments I have just described. Only then can you understand me and my story, and perhaps unfold its meaning.

I remember like it was yesterday that moment when I caught my first glimpse of Charis, glimmering in the distance. Initially I thought the remote city seemed cold, even oppressive. Our band of travelers that day had rounded a bend shaded by rock towers, and there it was, off to the west, rising high on a ridge. Silently, we all stared at it.

From where we stood, all we could see between us and the mountain crowned by Charis were rolling green hills scrawled with various pathways, including a ribbon of red. This was the "red road" I'd first learned of in some ancient inscriptions in a cave I'd entered one evening to escape a pounding rain and crashing thunderstorm—and something far worse. But that's another story, to tell another time.

As my traveling companions and I continued absorbing our first glimpse of the faraway city on the summit, it took only a moment for my heightened vision to pierce its walls. How did this happen? I can't explain it, but I was as certain of my perception as I could be. My intuition told me that the light was but a ruse, that inside the city all was dank and shadowy. And enthroned there sat a dreadful, intolerant tyrant, squashing creativity and initiative, enslaving any subjects foolish enough to enter the city. I envisioned him granting his slaves freedom enough to make a mistake just so he could condemn them for it and command their execution.

I'd long ago learned to trust my instincts, which had helped make me such a successful businessman and entrepreneur. And those prized instincts assured me this city was a monument to the pride of some self-proclaimed, glory-hungry sovereign who delighted in robbing men of their dignity. A strangely confident assessment for one who knew so little. But if I lacked something in those days, it was not confidence.

As this insight percolated within me, our silence was broken by one of my companions—a white-haired, craggy-faced man they called Shadrach, dressed in a tattered toga. "Behold," he said, air moving through a gap in his teeth, "Charis, the City of Light."

Light? What about the shadows I felt certain lay within? How could that old geezer be fool enough to trust that light on the outside meant light within?

Then suddenly another traveler, a young African woman named Malaiki, her face glowing, gasped, "Do you hear it? *Music!*"

I heard nothing. Who was she trying to trick, and why?

With enchanting fervor Malaiki exclaimed, "Songs of life and learning, choruses of pleasure and adventure! In a thousand languages!" She broke into dancing, soon joined by some of the others.

Were they trying to make fools of themselves? The uncomfortable thought struck me that perhaps I envied them, wishing I had a reason to dance. I quickly pushed the thought away.

Even as they twirled and high-stepped, they kept looking toward the city. Following their gaze, I found my perception changing, despite my resistance. The coldness of the place was gradually replaced by light and warmth and by what seemed to be the radiant energy of people celebrating. The city began to shimmer on the horizon, touched by sparkling blues and greens and golds that blended with the sky and sunlight, pulsing in and out of my vision.

Soon I, too, could hear music from the city and then what sounded like a geyser of laughter exploding from a fountain of joy.

My traveling comrades went on to speak of Charis as the city of a certain king whom they described in fantastic language. But my ingrained skepticism welled up and overtook me again. How could they make such claims? For reasons I couldn't grasp, I refused to let myself fall in with these people or be drawn to this city that enchanted them. I could not surrender control of my life's journey or its destination. I was master of my fate and captain of my soul. Besides, I reminded myself, I knew of someone who could take me elsewhere, to a better place.

I'd met Joshua on the morning I stumbled out of that cave, when I'd wandered in a daze, not knowing where I was. I started running, and as I came into an oak grove, a man bounded in my direction. He was tall, muscular, and handsome, with a neatly trimmed copper beard. He wore sandals and an emerald toga, cinched at his slender waist with a braided red cord. Though his dress was like a statesman's from another era, he somehow appeared modern and fashionable.

"Welcome, Nick," he called in a rich, clear voice, smiling broadly.

I wanted to grill him with a dozen questions, starting with, "How do you know my name?" and "Where are we?" and "How did I get here?" But I didn't want to reveal too much about myself and my ignorance.

"Call me Joshua," he said, extending his arm. I was struck by the strength of his grip. I couldn't help staring into his eyes—morning-glory eyes, radiant blue windows of experience and knowledge and promise, deep-set eyes a person could get lost in.

He invited me to join a group of travelers he was with, but at the time I preferred to go farther on my own. Joshua put his arm around me. "Go if you must," he said, giving me a solemn look. "But be careful whom you trust." This country, he explained, was beautiful but not safe.

Here was a man with inside information, and I wanted to know what he knew. Still, for some reason, I held back from asking him. As I turned to go on my way, Joshua smiled broadly and waved his great right arm, bronzed and powerful.

Soon I met him again, after I'd joined another group—the travelers on the red road who'd shared with me that first faraway glimpse of Charis. The old man Shadrach—who seemed overly confident about what was true and what wasn't—had warned me against nearly everything I found interesting, including spending time with Joshua. But by then I wasn't sure about the red road and where it led, and I certainly wasn't sure I wanted to stay in the company of those travelers, Shadrach in particular. I told Joshua, "I'd like to check out some other options."

"I'd be happy to serve as your guide," he answered. He led me off the red road and down a series of roads that were gray—roads that promised me all the things I'd ever wanted.

When we first set out, Joshua pointed ahead and told me, "Lead the way, my friend." Though he was my guide, he showed me respect by walking to my side, a step behind me, giving me a sense of control. I liked that.

I was in conquer mode, so we marched down the terrain at a fast clip. It was a plunging path at first, filled with sharp turns and lined with thornbushes that kept nipping at my pant legs. After an hour, we hadn't reached a single rise in the trail.

"Does this path only go down?" I asked.

Joshua laughed and answered, "To the very heart of things!"

The path kept descending, and our pace kept accelerating.

Finally, after dropping into a treacherous bog, we came to an intersecting path that rose upward toward firmer ground. Reaching the top of a slope and emerging from some trees, I came to a halt. Before me, positioned amid a half-dozen towering spires of rock, stood a glass and granite high-rise building. The sight of it was dreamlike yet so vivid, down to every detail. As I walked toward the structure, heart pounding, I stopped abruptly. This was the office building where I worked! I'd never seen it like this, isolated from the surrounding cityscape, as if it had been uprooted by some alien power and transported here.

I entered the familiar ground-level front door with Joshua a step behind. We took the elevator to the twenty-fifth floor, and I instinctively walked through the maze of work stations toward my corner office. Joshua gazed approvingly at the view through the windows beside us. "You belong here, don't you?" he asked me.

I nodded. This was my world, and I had sailed its waters and directed my subordinates as expertly as any sea captain had ever commanded his ship and his men.

Inside my office, Joshua said with a gesture of his hand, "This is what you were made for, isn't it?"

Before I could answer, my attention was drawn to a photograph on the desk, a picture of my wife and two children. It had been taken three years earlier, when we still lived together. I hadn't been able to get away from the office that day to make the appointment at the studio, but my wife told the photographer to take the picture anyway. "It's more realistic with just the three of us," she said to me later, twisting the knife.

Joshua and I left the office. But after stepping off the elevator and out the front door, everything went out of focus—until I suddenly found myself with Joshua in my condo, listening to classical music. The absence of transition made me think I must be dreaming, yet I was completely lucid, and my blue recliner was as tangible as could be, right down to the little coffee stain on the right arm.

For a few hours, I was immersed in a whirlpool of melancholy and reflection, going wherever the melodies led, over the mountains and valleys and through the deserts of my life. Especially the deserts.

"The music's beautiful, isn't it?" Joshua said.

"Yes. Beautiful."

I followed him as he walked down a hallway lined on one side with oak shelves filled with books. "Commendable," Joshua commented as he pulled out volumes here and there. "You have a genuine thirst for truth."

He fixed those radiant blue eyes on me. "You can find what you seek on one of the roads traveled by the great minds. Choose any of them. I'll take you there in an instant. And if you don't like one of them, I'll take you to the next and then the next."

I shook my head, believing there was something more I wanted, something no great thinker could lead me to.

No sooner had I turned down this offer than we materialized back on a gray road. Before us stood more buildings rising up from the rocks and sagebrush. We entered a maze of mall interiors, where my eyes were drawn to displays of home theaters, power tools, antique guns, shiny knives, snow skis, camping gear, sports clothing. We looked over a balcony to see spotlights zooming over showroom floors filled with the latest-model cars and pickup trucks, boats and RVs, snowmobiles and motorcycles.

Then the spotlights melted into marquee lights. Joshua and I walked into a fine restaurant filled with people in fine clothes drinking fine wines. My heart suddenly buoyed when I saw a woman alone at one of the tables, a woman who'd been part of the group of travelers I was with earlier. She looked so beautiful tonight, so slight and delicate, dressed so elegantly. I studied every inch of her. The longer I looked, the more she filled my heart.

"Go sit with her," Joshua suggested. He led me by the arm and took me to her table, then excused himself. "I have other things to take care of."

The woman seemed pleased to see me. We dined alone and toasted with champagne. When the music began, we danced. I felt intoxicated.

She kissed me, then smiled and said she had to go.

"Can I...go with you?"

"Not tonight," she whispered, but she smiled as she walked away, and her eyes said yes.

TWO

Joshua walked up beside me and motioned me down a high-ceilinged corridor, then toward a tinted-glass doorway, where other men were entering. I followed.

Inside the building it was hot and sticky. A foul odor turned my stomach. An army of nipping black flies buzzed around me. At first I swatted at them, but there were so many I finally gave up.

The stench overwhelmed me, and I fell to my knees, nearly vomiting.

But the next moment I felt fine, alive, energized, eager to move ahead. The foul odor was gone, and instead I smelled sweet perfume.

Through arched doorways I could see the women. I breathed deeply the perfumed air. It was glorious. My thoughts were on one thing only. I was hypnotized, like a moth fluttering around a blinding light. My longing increased until I knew I would sell my soul for the promised pleasures. I was awash in a tidal wave of passion.

Suddenly pain shot through my torso and up into my head like a runaway train. I reeled from the blow and tried to shake it off me. The pain was dreadful. But I continued my quest despite it, obsessed with what I wanted.

I looked around at the other men, all of us indulging, none of us satisfied. Some of the men frantically redirected their longings, men looking upon men or even upon children. In a feeding frenzy we became predators, consumers of others, cannibals, no longer men but obscene appetites.

It became a prison riot, and I was in the thick of it. I was ashamed, but my shame gave me no power to resist. I felt helpless, like a junkie enslaved to his addiction.

Another wild rush of pain overwhelmed me, a throbbing ache that deepened my emptiness. And the emptiness demanded to be filled. I entered beneath an archway, then another and another. I moved from place to place, indulging more and more, satisfied less and less. Still I came back for more.

As I entered one last archway, I didn't find what I expected. I saw my own wife—but I didn't know who she was. Not really. I'd never stopped to ask her. I'd used her as one more object, one more possession, one more hunting trophy.

I gazed up at swaying women on a stage. A shock wave assailed me, followed by a sick emptiness. I heard myself scream in horror. Why? My own daughter had joined the parading women on stage.

In the din, no one else heard me scream.

I gazed into the emptiness of my daughter's eyes. I started pushing and shoving. I wanted to kill the men who lusted after her—vile men whose daughters I'd lusted after.

Something happened in that moment. In seeing my little girl, I saw my wife and the other women as they really were—frightened daughters and hardened mothers, desperate souls projecting images of delighted sensuality when inside they felt nothing but disdain for the men and themselves. The raging lust in my blood chilled to shame.

I sobbed hopelessly, then finally ran out through the tinted-glass doors and down city blocks of gnawing emptiness, collapsing in a heap.

I looked up to see Joshua. He stepped forward, smiling. "Come," he said softly. "There's much more to see."

Before I knew it, we were walking into a lush hotel hallway. Joshua hesitated, looking as if he'd intended for us to go elsewhere.

Gilded elevator doors opened across the hall. Out stepped a well-dressed businessman accompanied by a woman with the face and figure of a man's dreams. They walked side by side down the hallway, laughing lightly in obvious anticipation.

I knew who they were and what was about to happen. I felt my stomach turn.

They slipped into the room, not seeming to notice us as we stood observing them. Then I watched as the fool torched solemn vows made twenty-five years before and threw ashes to the wind.

"Stop!" I cried. "Don't you see what you're doing?" He couldn't hear me, or wouldn't.

Suddenly I saw the dropping blade of a guillotine, spilling my blood on the clean sheets of a luxury hotel bed. I saw the face of the woman of my dreams after a night of blind passion, when beauty faded and she became demanding and ugly, one more dried-up carcass in this great web, a revolting reminder of my own condition.

Then I saw the worst of it, hidden from me until that moment. The drama, everything I'd just seen, was being acted out on a stage—and in the audience sat my wife. She stared at us, at me and the other woman. She silently watched my betrayal, watched me violate my vows, watched the ugly procession of the lies I had become. I saw her sobs, her grief, her anger, and then watched as her face hardened against me, against life itself.

I called her name and cried out, "I'm sorry, I didn't mean to hurt you!" She couldn't hear me. Too little, too late.

Just when I thought nothing could be more horrible, I saw my two children seated beside their mother, witnessing the same ugliness, watching their father weave his own web of deceit. They saw me embrace this woman in our "secret" hotel room that was on center stage of the universe.

The truth is, I was later instructed, there's no such thing as a private moment; the whole cosmos is our audience for everything we do in the dark.

I cried out to my son and daughter, "No, you don't

understand. It wasn't like that. It wasn't as bad as it appears." But everyone in that cosmic auditorium knew the truth was *exactly* as it appeared. My children could see right through me, right through the traitor they'd once loved and now despised. I saw the stunned looks on their faces, the disgust, the brooding anger. I felt the heart-stab of their hurt and confusion. I watched them turn from me.

"I'm sorry!" I spoke the words I'd never said to them before.

I watched them recklessly run away from the auditorium. I knew they were going to choose their own wrong roads—because the man they'd trusted was a turncoat and a liar and a cheat. Worse yet, what dwelt in their father had lodged itself deep within them as well.

If there is a hell, was I there already?

I turned away and ran, hearing the sound of clanging metal in my pocket, too frightened to reach in and discover what it was.

I ran and ran, not knowing what direction I was going, my eyes blinded by tears and wind, trying to outrun my shame. Finally I collapsed beside the brackish water of a scum-covered pond.

What I'd experienced on the gray roads had only left me more thirsty and more sick, as if I'd drunk salt water when I craved fresh.

As I lay on the ground, I looked up to a plum tree, where a large gray owl perched on a low branch and studied me. He swiveled his head back and forth without blinking, as if scanning me curiously. His implied question seemed the same as mine—who was I anyway? Who was Nick Seagrave?

The owl suddenly looked behind me, and I turned to see Joshua walking toward me. I rose to my feet, trying not to appear as weak as I felt.

"If there's nowhere else to go," I told him, "I'll return to the red road." Though I'd told myself the other roads had more to offer, at least on the red road I'd sometimes sensed what couldn't be found here—reason for hope.

"There are other places," Joshua said, his voice full of optimism. "Lots of them. Don't give up."

He suggested I try "roads of religion." *No,* I thought. *Those aren't for me.* "What about roads of spirituality?" he asked. *Yes, that sounded better.* Before I realized what was happening, he'd led me to an overlook, and we gazed down onto a dusty plain with gulches here and there. Countless roads led out into the distance, as many roads as there were directions. Some fell into the gulches, others went farther toward the horizon.

"They all have something that will benefit you," Joshua said.

"Is it possible to find...the truth?" I asked him.

"That's a lifelong pursuit. You need to look far and wide to find bits of truth you can weave all together into something that satisfies you."

He smiled. "Forward," he urged me.

Forward. But to where? To which road? Was there such a

thing as truth? Would one of these roads take me there? I felt a glimmer of hope. Was I right to hope? Or was I just a fool?

Joshua led me to a deep canal and, beside it, a three-sided wooden building, open in the front, with candles, incense, books, altars, and offering boxes on display. Inside, a quiet group of worshipers stood or knelt.

We approached a man in a red robe, meditating in the lovely silence.

"Which religion is true?" I asked him, whispering as if I didn't want to admit the question was mine. "And how can we know?"

"We practice all religions here," he said, "for we see truth in all of them."

"How do I know what to embrace and what to reject?"

"Embrace what you wish and reject what you wish. It's yours to choose."

"I understand it's all my choice, but what I mean is, what *should* I choose?"

"You should choose only what you wish. We won't force anything on you."

"Yes, yes, I know you won't force me, but…I'm looking for *truth.*"

"Commendable," the man said, nodding wisely. "There's truth in all religions, in all spiritual traditions. You must choose your own truth."

I threw my hands up and walked away, wondering if I was insane or if the man in the red robe was. Shaking my head in frustration, I kicked the dust with my boot.

Joshua had disappeared for the moment, but a man with a square jaw, a Middle Eastern complexion, and long, jet-black hair approached me and easily began a conversation. He seemed to sense my frustration. As we talked, I mentioned how lately, when walking the red road, I'd been able at times to observe what I never had before—"to see into other worlds. It's as if I've been given eyes that see what isn't there!"

"Or is it that your eyes now see what was there all along?"

"Seeing is believing," I answered. "If you can't sense it, it isn't real."

"In a world where seeing is believing," he responded, "men believe much that is not true. And they disbelieve much that is true."

His eyes scanned the great plain spread out before us, full of people walking on the various roads. His gaze pulled mine with it, and I saw a hundred red-winged blackbirds in sudden flight, appearing to flee from something I couldn't see.

The plain suddenly transformed into an immense battle-field. I quickly recognized two opposing forces. On one side were great gladiators with eyes of fire, warriors from the bright city of the west. Lifting swords against them were soldiers with cold shark eyes—dark warriors from the realms of gray.

Some of the fighting took place on the ground and some above it, as if the air had an invisible floor. Sparks flew from clashing swords, and lightning bolts pierced the sky as thunderclaps exploded.

Meanwhile, the people I'd seen earlier on the gray roads continued walking on the ground underneath the great combatants. They appeared translucent now, almost invisible. Most of them stepped casually, unguardedly, utterly unaware of the battle raging above and around them—yet they, too, were being assaulted by the gray warriors.

Behind and above me came a flapping sound. I turned to see a monstrous carrion fowl plunging at me. I ran as he circled again and came from behind. More beast than bird, he dived and pursued me, coming this way and that, as if he was herding me somewhere. Before I knew it, I found myself on the plain, in the thick of battle.

Arrows shot past me. Then I heard a *swoosh* and felt something pierce my left shoulder. I saw the arrow just before I felt the pain, as lightning before thunder. I screamed in agony.

I fell to the ground, looking for help but seeing none. I clasped both hands around the shaft and pulled, screaming as the arrowhead tore the flesh that had closed around it.

I swooned, the pain threatening to sweep me into unconsciousness. I opened my eyes to see a powerful warrior standing over me, his face contorted. He raised a sword high, like an executioner. I froze, held by pain and fear. He brought down the sword, and I saw it glimmer in the sunlight only a moment before it sliced into my right arm, just above my elbow. Waves of convulsing agony ushered me into the darkness.

THREE

Warm blood from my shoulder wound awakened me—or maybe it was the deep cut above my elbow that screamed for attention. I tried to stop the bleeding, but my right arm hung limp and useless.

Where was the enemy who'd cut me? Why hadn't he finished me off?

Twenty feet away stood the answer. Battling my attacker was another great warrior—I saw only his back and his jet-black hair dangling halfway down it.

Surprisingly lucid considering my pain, I lay still, trying to bind my wounds with strips of my torn shirt. Clanging sounds of battle surrounded me.

The shark-eyed monster slammed to the ground the black-haired warrior who'd defended me. Shark eyes, who'd sliced my arm, now raised his sword and laughed sadistically as he swung it down toward my head.

My bodyguard, immediately back on his feet, stepped forward and swung his sword horizontally, deflecting the enemy's blow so it missed my head, instead slicing a quarter inch of flesh off my left forearm. Howling at the white-hot pain, I tried to clutch the wound with my limp right hand.

In a cloud of combat dust, I crawled to lower ground. Helpless, with no way to defend myself, I could only lie hurting and watch. The people on the ground, walking the roads, still seemed oblivious to the battle. Many of them fell beneath blows from the dark warriors—some screaming, yet others perishing with no more than a groan or whimper. How could they be oblivious to the cosmic battle with them at stake? How could I have been oblivious to it until now?

Trembling at the fierce warfare around me, I lay low. As I looked from east to west, I became aware of two gigantic commanders at opposite ends of the valley. My gaze was drawn inescapably to the commander of the dark army, shark eyes set deep in his contorted face. Cruelty sprang from his eyes like smoke and fire from cannons. He gloated and taunted, cursing the air above and the ground beneath. He fired flaming arrows and poisoned darts into people who did nothing to protect themselves.

My heart stopped when he turned and noticed me watching. He stared at me like a stalker. His eyes flashed, and for a moment my skin seemed to burn under the napalm of his hatred. Why was he looking at me when countless others filled the battlefield?

He hoisted a gigantic harpoon and pointed it directly at me. Just as he threw it, I rolled and heard an explosive sound as it cut through the air with hideous fury. It passed only inches from me, then grazed the black-haired warrior by my side. My defender cried out and touched his left leg, but stood his ground seeking to position himself between me and my murderous enemy.

Panicked, I got up and ran, stumbling, unsure where to go.

Looking back, I saw the dark lord open his mouth in mocking laughter, a sound so thunderous it rose above the roar of battle. Then he swung bolas round and round in the air, keeping his eyes on me. When I could hardly stand the sight of one more circle of those metal balls, he released the weapon. It flew, freezing my blood at the sight of it coming. It hit my legs and wrapped itself around me. I lost balance and braced myself for the fall. I heard the sickening crunch of my own bones. The bola beat me to the ground, pummeling me even after I fell.

I could hardly breathe. Broken and bleeding, I knew I would surely die.

The mighty beast, Shark Eyes, glared at me and then marched across the valley, taking huge strides forward, carrying a battle-ax.

I tried to crawl away but couldn't. My head in the dirt, a flood of images raced through my mind, images of a broken life I would never have a chance to fix.

Just then I heard a great voice speaking a language I couldn't understand. I turned to see the bright commander also marching toward me, from the opposite end of the valley. His face was a rock, his chin set and resolute. He seemed far more human than the beast, yet not human at all—just not the fallen animal that was his counterpart. The powerful warrior of light kept returning his eyes to me. They were loyal and kind, yet burning with an unquenchable fire. He did not scream or gloat; he strode unflinchingly toward me, matching the movement of the beast.

Somehow it dawned on me that these two beings were once of the same race, the greatest of their kind, before something dark and terrible had happened. The beast watched his ancient brother and foe come forward to take his meal from him—for I was nothing now but a meal. Outraged at the insolence of the warrior of light, the beast raised his fists to the sky. He hissed long and hard, then screamed,

"Baal jezeb ashnar mordol nuhl—keez gimbus molech nargul dazg!"

He spit the words, as if he could not bear their weight on his tongue. I reeled backward at this dark language. My vision blackened; I groped for sight, gasping for breath, for the foulness of the ancient words had torn all goodness out of the sky.

The great warrior, his eyes living and ablaze, the tendons of his great neck stretched, stared at the evil prince, then raised his right fist and cried to the sky, "Elyon miriel o aeron galad—chara domina beth charis o aleathes celebron!"

His speech was loud as a deafening waterfall, yet the words pure as refined gold and sweet as honey. The raging beast covered his ears, wincing and shouting vile foreign slurs in a fruitless attempt to drown out the cascading echo of the golden words. I heard a multitude of unseen warriors above take up the words of their general, the commander of untold millions. The warrior's glad shout became a mighty song.

I felt he was coming to rescue me, and I longed for it. Yet I did not know whether, should he take hold of me, I would fare better in his holy hands than I would in the evil hands of his dark counterpart.

But suddenly the Warrior stopped in his tracks, then looked up to the sky as if listening to someone's voice. Was it his commander-in-chief? Who was so great that he could supervise such a one as this?

Shark Eyes marched on, gloating and energized when he saw his enemy stop. Without the warrior of light to stop him, the dark beast would surely tear me to pieces and grind me into the dirt beneath his feet.

My briefly enjoyed moments of hope had disappeared. My spirit felt trapped in frozen flesh. In what I felt certain would be my final seconds of life, in moments that would have seemed far too short to have done so, I became strangely contemplative about this ancient war I had witnessed for the first time.

The conflicting missions of the two armies seemed to have no gray, only absolute black-and-white clarity. I had lived my life in compromise, rule bending, trade-offs, concessions, and bargaining. I had been a deal-striker, a finder of middle ground.

But in these two great armies, embodied in their two champions, there was no such thing. Good was good; evil was evil. The warriors shared a common beginning, for a time a common history, but at one decisive point choices between light and darkness had been made, choices that meant they could never again share common ground. I had beheld no more tolerance for malice and evil in the eyes of the great shining warrior than I had seen tolerance for goodness and grace in the eyes of the dreadful beast.

Though my body was racked with pain, my thoughts stayed clear and focused. I looked around again at the little people so pathetically oblivious to the battle. They seemed to fancy themselves neutral and at peace, hoping to maintain dual citizenship in the two warring kingdoms. I was shocked at their ignorance, stunned at their indifference to the gravity and stakes of this ferocious cosmic war. Above all, I felt crushed to realize that all my life I'd been just like them, every bit as blind as they. But now, in moments of perfect and frightening lucidity, I had seen reality just as it was. And that reality had shown not the slightest signs of subtlety. Not a hint of any nuances, tones, or shading. It was what it was. And what it was would never be altered by wishes or pleas or curses or popular vote.

These settled thoughts crystallized within me in a period of but a few seconds. No sooner and no later had they done so, than I turned toward the hideous face of the dark commander, now but thirty feet from me. As I thrashed about, I was struck by the irony that the greatest moments of clarity I'd ever known would now culminate in my slaughter. I would have welcomed death, but I had a horrible feeling that what awaited me on the other side was something far worse than oblivion.

The beast raised his fearsome battle-ax above my head. Trembling, I looked into the shark eyes of my gloating executioner.

The ax fell. But just as it came upon me, Shark Eyes disappeared. The Shining Warrior disappeared. All the combatants from both sides disappeared. The people on the plain popped back into normal view, as solid as the warriors had been the moment before.

Silence.

I lifted my head from the dirt and looked side to side. It took me a moment to realize the pain in my shoulder and arms and chest had disappeared, replaced by an aching void within me, an internal pain not as excruciating as the external one I'd just been delivered of, but every bit as real.

I looked around, relieved at the appearance of things. All seemed peaceful. There was no battle. At least no battle I could see.

Once more, the square-jawed man with long black hair approached me. He dripped with sweat, haggard and limping, favoring his left leg.

"What happened?" I asked, but before he could answer, he appeared to burst into flames that did not consume him but left his features still visible. My face blistered at the heat. Then a portal opened in midair, giving me a moment's glimpse of something beyond. His face glowing white hot, grimacing and resolute, like a soldier headed back to battle, the black-haired warrior marched alone, limping through the portal to the universe next door.

When he'd vanished, I ran my hands over my body again, barely able to believe my wounds were gone and I could move freely. I stood slowly, then dizzily sank back down to the ground and clutched the dirt, closing my eyes. At first I was sure I would never forget what had happened. Then I tried to remember it. Everything was so clear. Rather, it *had been* so clear just a few minutes ago. As I faded into sleep I tried to latch on to whatever it was that I had come to see, that was so important and I had been determined never to forget. It seemed like air escaping slowly from an inner tube.

It was dark when I awoke. I got up slowly, knees creaking, neck stiff. Hearing a crackling sound, I peered through tree branches and saw a fire in the distance. I walked to it and found Joshua sitting there, staring into the flames.

"Good to see you again," he told me.

I studied his face, sculpted and powerful and kind. He looked remarkably like someone I had just seen. Who was it? It must be the commander of the bright army. For a moment I felt certain it was him. I almost asked Joshua why he'd stopped, why he hadn't defended me against the dark lord.

"Have something to eat; then go back to sleep," he said in a reassuring voice. "Tomorrow I have something to show you."

FOUR

Joshua served a delicious breakfast, then told me, "I have others who need my guidance now. I must go to them, but I'll return in a few hours. Just find some shade and relax. I'll be back. Will you be all right?"

I nodded and watched him walk into some thick vine maples, a rich tapestry of fall colors. He disappeared.

Later, alone, I climbed a hill. Glancing down, I was surprised to see a huge figure, a giant in a flowing black robe, standing on the hillside, looking down over the roads. Instinctively, I ducked behind a large willow tree and watched as the breeze parted the branches just enough for me to see.

As I hid, random thoughts assaulted me. Among them was my father spending his life affirming his independence, then slowly dying without so much as control over his bladder, as clueless about the world he lived in as about the worlds beyond.

The ominous black-robed being cast a long shadow across the hillside, and when he moved and the shadow fell over others of the little people, I heard howls and whimpers. The man—or was he a great beast—stood smiling, gloating, taking pleasure in the pain he saw on the roads below him. He took out a lyre and played music and sang an otherworldly song. It sounded compelling, yet at moments seemed like a fraud, a counterfeit of some truer and deeper song. He laughed and pointed his finger at the sprawling misery and played his music like a cosmic Nero, fiddling while a world burned.

He blew smoke out his nose. Then, to my horror, I saw him putting little people into his mouth. He smoked men as if they were cigarettes. Soon he had a half dozen in at once, a macabre sight that turned my stomach and made my knees tremble. He wheezed and choked and laughed like a junior high boy indulging in a forbidden vice.

When he was done, he crumpled the human cigarettes one by one, slowly, as if taking exquisite pleasure in the undoing of each. Finally, he tossed them to the ground. I watched him lift his leg, the leg of a tyrannosaur, and smash them, grinding them until they were flat. Even then he didn't stop grinding.

Throat tight, I shivered in the shade of the willow.

I knew him. I'd seen him on the great battlefield with a raised battle-ax, attempting to remove my head and nearly succeeding. Even at a distance I could see his shark eyes. I chilled at his singing.

At the same moment, I heard another song in the air, a song in the distance like a pale but ever-growing light behind a dark curtain of rain. It was a melody in the wind blowing gently from Charis, City of Light, barely visible in the west. It was a song of love and might, of grace and victory.

The dark prince put his hands over his ears and yelled curses, pacing back and forth. I wondered how such a bright song could be sung in the presence of such cruel evil. Yet it wafted its way through the miserable air of the dead-end roads below, reverberating even in the sewer drains that connected them. I saw people here and there on various roads responding to it, smiling, then turning to walk up the hillside to the red road.

The dark prince called to the people, in a smooth and inviting voice that belied his beastly form. "That song is a lie! You'd be fools to believe it. I have better ways, better roads, and lots of them. Choose what you like, decide what you wish to be true. Let me show you. Come my way! Follow me there!"

He sounded like a carnival barker inviting men into his house of mirrors.

A gust of wind blew back the willow branches in front of me, and suddenly he turned and saw me watching him. He seemed surprised, and angry to see me. My blood froze. As I looked on helplessly, he stepped off the hillside as gracefully as a hang glider, his body transforming into a flying beast, a hell hawk, claws grasping the air.

He flew toward the willow and circled over me. I saw the weathered scales of his underside. I was overwhelmed by the putrid smell of ancient, rotting flesh, caked with blood and

desiccated human body parts. I saw on the scales of this filthy, gluttonous beast the dried residue of his sickening drool.

The thunderclaps of his flapping wings deafened me. He parted his razor teeth and descended. I choked on malevolence, strangled by doom. Just as the beast opened his mouth, just as I smelled his wretched breath, his head yanked backward, and he disappeared.

Why had I been delivered from him again? And why did I feel so certain this rescue would be my last?

Disoriented, I sat there, catching my breath, seeking to shake the terror. Finally I walked out from under the willow branches feeling as if space and time had turned inside out.

A familiar figure walked toward me, returning from his obligations.

"Joshua!"

I smiled and walked toward him. I extended my hand. When I got close I caught the faint scent of sulfur. I looked at his face, then recoiled, standing for a moment in stunned silence.

Joshua's face was a mask with two holes. His eyes were not radiant blue. They were the dark, dull eyes of a shark!

I turned and ran until I could run no farther. I found shelter at the hollow base of an old tree, crawled in, and covered my twitching face.

urled up in that tree hollow, I dared not emerge until I knew Joshua couldn't find me. Suddenly, I felt as if a giant spider lurked behind me. Forcing myself to look up, I let out my breath when I saw the familiar face of a white-haired man in a ragged toga—Shadrach, the gap-toothed traveler from the red road. He saw me trembling with fear.

"I tried to warn you about him," Shadrach said in his gravelly voice.

"Why didn't you?" I stammered.

"You wouldn't listen. It was as if you couldn't hear my words."

It was true. I'd never seen Shadrach as anything but a smelly, weathered old fool who rattled on and on about nonsense. I remembered how he would corner me and say, "I must tell you about the *chasm*"—some vast abyss that he said separated road-walkers from Charis. It was spooky talk, and I brushed him off, but it bothered me enough that I had asked Joshua about it.

"There is no chasm," he had answered. "Even if there were, it's the last place you'd want to go." That settled the issue for me at the time. But now I'd seen who Joshua was. And it made everything he'd said to me suspect.

"This time," the old man went on, as if reading my thoughts, "he could not keep you from seeing him as he really is. But don't underestimate him. He won't give up."

I had no words to speak—I was trying to process it all.

The old man pointed to the edge of a nearby valley, not far from where I'd seen Joshua stomping out men like cigarettes. "Look at the image-bearers who have forgotten who they are." I watched their trancelike movements, zombies following the crowd.

He turned to me. "You're one of those, are you not? The Impostor gives them wrong dreams or robs them of the right ones—it's all the same. He gives them hope in the wrong things, then takes away their hope in the right ones. Like a cruel, fastidious nanny, he scrubs the hope out of their bloodshot eyes."

"It's not what I want," I said.

"Be grateful you can return to the red road, for few men get so many chances as you have." Looking about him, he lectured me about this "hollow cavern of broken promises and abandoned dreams." But he also spoke of the great King in Charis and of his fight against a gloating pretender who was powerless against the King, except for the power granted him at that very King's discretion.

I remembered the conflict that I'd witnessed briefly but so horrifically on the plain.

"Then why the great battle?" I asked. "And why is evil winning?"

"Not all questions can be answered now," the old man replied mysteriously. He looked at me intently. "And not all is as it appears. Are you ready to walk the red road to the chasm?"

"I want to go to Charis—I can tell you that much." Even as I said it, the words struck me, as if I'd finally spoken what I knew deep in my heart. "If the red road will take me there, it's the red road I want. As for the chasm, I'm still not convinced there is one. And if there is, why would I want to go there?"

"It isn't a matter of wanting. No one *wants* the chasm to be there. But we don't get a vote—or, rather, we all cast our votes long ago. You can go to the chasm directly by walking the red road, where you can face it while you're still alive. Or you can waste your life walking the other roads that avoid the chasm for the moment. But then, when all opportunity to deal with it is past, they dump you there the instant you die."

He turned and pointed to a sharp incline of rocks and shale above. "Follow me," he said. "We must climb up to that ledge."

"It's halfway up the mountain!"

"Yes. It leads to a higher point on the red road, and it will afford us the view you need. Once you see the roads and the landscape from above, you'll understand."

Part of me resisted going with him, but I felt certain there was no future elsewhere. The red road might or might not be a dead end—but everything else I'd seen certainly was.

I followed the old man, surprised that he negotiated the mountain like a goat. If I hadn't put my feet in the same places he put his, I would have fallen a dozen times. I pushed myself to keep up with him.

We climbed for perhaps eight hours with little rest. The old man kept the lead and reached the top well ahead of me.

"This is the red road," he called down to me, still twenty feet below.

I scrambled up the last stretch, stepped out on the ledge, and took in a sight that stole my breath away. It was a canyon so large that it stretched out against the horizon as far as I could see. Way in the distance, on the other side, was the City of Light, appearing much farther away than before.

I looked down at all the other roads, the gray roads. They circled and meandered until each one finally emptied at some point into the chasm, each at a different spot. On each road I could see tiny dots that I supposed were people or groups of people. I could see how the roads wound around so much that they gave the illusion of progress and afforded no view of the chasm. But from here, high above, the picture was radically different.

I have brought you now to where my story began. Perhaps you begin to understand the desperation with which I looked at that chasm. And why it seemed the end of all life, the end of all hope. To stay on this side of the chasm and walk the dead-end roads, to give myself still more false hopes and only feed the gnawing emptiness within and wait for death to sweep me away... it seemed unthinkable. But what was the alternative? To cross the chasm and make it to the City of Light was impossible.

I turned back to old Shadrach and said, "The red road goes to the chasm like all the other roads."

"Yes, I told you that," he said crossly. "And I also told you, did I not, that the red road takes you to the chasm *before* you die, not after?"

"What difference does that make? It's all the same in the end."

"No. It makes all the difference. You will see. That is, if you choose to go there with me."

I considered my options. I stared down at the winding, wandering gray roads below, the cul-de-sacs, the figure eights, the circles—all going nowhere.

Heading toward a chasm didn't appear to make sense—but I refused to go back to where I'd been.

I looked at the shining city on the mountain beyond the chasm. Was Charis the home I'd never known but always longed for?

Maybe it made no sense to walk toward this chasm—but so be it. If a thousand things that made sense to me had turned out wrong, perhaps this thing that didn't make sense would turn out right. If the only way to escape this country was to walk to the chasm, what else was I to do? Perhaps the chasm had a floor, not visible from here, that could be traveled. It would take every ounce of strength I could muster to cross it. But maybe I could do it after all. I'd done many things others didn't think I could. This much I knew—that shimmering vision beyond the chasm…that place called Charis…was where I had to be.

"Let's go," I said. "I'm walking the red road."

t took us most of the day to descend the mountain. At its base, it became barren desert—nothing but rock, sand, and salt flats.

I fingered a few cactuses that had been cut wide open, robbed of their water stores by thirsty travelers. They were hard as truck tires.

We passed a lone mesquite tree, its roots deep, squeezing some hidden drops of moisture out of the rocky ground.

The only rises in the desert were mounds of formless slag surrounded by oily black ooze that emitted pungent fumes.

I could no longer see the chasm. I began to wonder if my eyes had played tricks on me up on the mountain. If it was really there and we were this close, I'd surely be able to see it, wouldn't I?

I looked in the distance at the shining city. I stared at it, feeling my heart ache when it shimmered out of sight even for a moment, then feeling revived when it reappeared. What was it really like there? I had to know. Nothing else mattered.

We camped for the night. In the darkness I heard wolves howling in the distance and eerie screams. I tossed and turned, tense and uneasy.

In the morning, we'd journeyed only a few hours when I began to smell something rank. The loathsome odor invaded my nostrils and gripped my stomach. Something terrible filled the air. Crook-necked vultures and unfamiliar birds of prey, hoary and weathered, circled above. They peered down expectantly. I couldn't escape the feeling that this vast stretch of land had fed their morbid appetites for millennia. Were we their next meal?

Suddenly I stopped dead and blinked my eyes. What had appeared to be level land stretching out into the distance now came into sharper focus. Before me was the very thing I'd seen from the mountaintop and hoped was an illusion. I had reached the chasm's mouth. It stretched farther than I could see with white rocks scattered around its pale, sandy rim.

I should have been prepared for this, but viewing the chasm from a distance was very different from seeing—and smelling— it at its edge. I was overwhelmed. There was no way to deny the chasm now. How could I have supposed for a moment it hadn't been there? It dominated the landscape. I turned my head, looking for some way around the abyss. But it was as wide as it was long.

As I walked the red road as far as it could take me, I saw that the fringes of the chasm were lined with corpses. I watched as reptilian carrion fowl feasted on human entrails, picking bones and pulling tendons with their great beaks. I recoiled at the sight. The stench of rotting flesh made me gag.

Upon closer inspection, I realized that what I at first thought were scattered white rocks in the sand were in fact human bones, picked clean by wind and sand and predators. The white sand was in fact powdered bone. The chasm before me was not some natural wonder, but an unnatural graveyard, unspeakably immense, with no tombstones or caretakers—nothing but the beating sun and the merciless winds of time.

The air was dry, yet thick with death, so thick I felt like I was breathing through a wet dishrag. Covering my nose and inhaling through my mouth as shallowly as I could, I stepped to the very edge of the chasm. I scanned it, wondering if there might yet be a way to descend and cross it.

What did the millions of human bones mean, scattered as far as I could see? Could it be that others before me—many no doubt smarter and stronger and better than I—had tried to find their way around and over and across the chasm?

Below me, the piles of bones scattered along the steep-sloped side of the chasm testified to the distances people had traveled. Though some had made it a few miles farther down the sheer edge than others—either by climbing skill or lengthy falls to their deaths—none had come close to crossing the

chasm. It was impossible even to *begin* to cross it. However long and deeply I gazed into it, I could see no hint of any ground to walk on.

It appeared to be a bottomless pit. And even if it wasn't... who could possibly cross it? And even if by some miracle they did...who could begin to climb the other side?

I *wanted* to cross it—but how could I?

I was jolted from my inner questioning by a sound. *What is that?* Haunting voices rising from the pit! But...how? The voices were faint yet distinct, full of sorrow and regret and bitterness and self-preoccupation. Voices of those who had no hope, who still had the longings of humanity but no possibility of fulfillment.

A chill pierced my bones. Did the voices come from the disembodied souls of the corpses and bones surrounding me? Were they voices of the damned?

A knot constricted my throat, and I gulped furiously for air. I fell to the ground as a sickening wave of terror welled up from my belly. I stretched out on the bone-powder sand, grabbing it with clenched fists. It sifted through my fingers. I could not hold the sands of death.

"It's hard to accept, isn't it?" a creaky voice asked. I lifted my head, brushing sand from my eyebrows. I looked up at the old man.

"I *don't* accept it," I said. "I can't. I won't."

I pulled myself up on one knee and gazed again at the abyss, at the battered remains of multitudes who had tried to cross. The more I stared, the more I clenched my teeth.

When I had turned from all the other roads, the roads of emptiness and delusion, I dared to hope the red road might be different. But here I was at death's end, robbed even of comforting illusions. At least the other roads, though they never led to Charis, offered diversions to occupy my time and anesthetize my aching heart. But the red road had ended here, offering nothing but hopeless despair. It had led me to the biggest dead end of all.

"If there's a king," I shouted, "why would he do this to us?"

"You blame the King?" the old man asked. "It wasn't he who made the chasm."

"Then who did?"

He stared at me. "We did." Then he pointed his bony finger. "*You* did."

I paced like an animal, fiercely resisting the absurd notion that I shared any blame for this infinite stretch of ruin. I felt sweat pooling on the bridge of my nose.

My eyes burned as if open in salt water. In my chest I felt the same tugging, the familiar longing that had pulled me down this road. But now the truth of the chasm had stripped me of hope. I knew the yearning could never be satisfied. I'd die as I had lived, lonely and disconnected. I would never enter Charis. The City of Light was nothing but a cruel joke—a comfort to the ignorant, an insult to the intelligent.

My body dropped like a sack of grain on rocky ground. The weight of worlds beyond fell upon me, and I collapsed.

Nothing mattered but the tragedy that gripped me. No one could change my destiny from chasm to Charis. The tears flowed—I didn't bother to wipe them. It was the darkest night of my soul.

SEVEN

The old man was nowhere to be seen now. I felt deserted. I had never been so alone.

But then, in a moment I shall never forget, I saw something in the distance. No, I saw some*one.* It was a human form walking toward me, as if stepping on the air above the chasm, where land should have been and perhaps once was, but no longer.

This dark-skinned man wore a white robe, but he was no ghost. Far from it. Somehow, he seemed more substantial, more human than I.

He walked straight to me and looked into my eyes, fixing his on mine. I didn't know him, but felt I should…as if everything I was seeking somehow led to him.

I sensed he knew me. I felt as if he'd come directly to my door, a messenger from far away, from a place he missed. I knew he had given up much to make his way to me.

He was a young man with ancient eyes. As I gazed into them, I caught a glimpse of what he had seen—a million worlds born and died. Wind-roughened and sun-darkened, the skin on his face was tough, like the sole of a boot. His white robe clung to him, stained with sweat and sawdust.

I saw in his eyes the explosions of thunderstorms, the collisions of galaxies. His dark yet white-hot eyes were wild—they hit me like a boxer's blows, swift and relentless.

He sang a beautiful melody, fresh and young, yet prehistoric—"I am here to do what must be done...and what no other can do...and what I can do no other way."

As he sang, my heart came alive. The song was so familiar, as if it had been sung within me always, but I could never identify the words until now. All my life, I'd been longing to hear that song, to understand it...to *sing* it.

Still, something held me back from this Woodsman. He looked so rough and ferocious...untamed and untamable.

The song was beautiful beyond imagination. But now he began to sing it in a minor key. He sang of rebellion and betrayal, of the chasm and blood and suffering and death. The same song that had drawn me to him now made me cringe.

I backed away from him, intrigued yet wary, doing battle with myself about who this really was and what claim he might make on me.

My heart sank as I looked toward where I'd last seen Charis. The chasm was still there, and I still had no way to cross it. Nothing had changed. As always, hope melted into disappointment, and I remembered why it was easier not to hope.

He walked toward me. There he stood, only three feet away, this solitary figure dressed in a plain old tunic, spotted with wood chips. He didn't look like a celebrity or a hero, just a wandering woodsman and perhaps a worker of wood. He gazed at the sprawling blue sky above us, then to Charis in the distance, as if looking toward home. In that moment, as though I were looking through his eyes, I saw Charis more clearly than I'd ever seen it.

He grabbed me with his eyes, holding me. I squirmed away from that hold and pointed my finger down at the chasm. Despair and anger welled up in me and exploded into a shouting challenge: "How can I cross the abyss? You demand the impossible! Is my longing for Charis your way of torturing me? Have you brought me here just to rub my face in misery?"

He followed my pointing finger and gazed down into the abyss. His eyes watered. I could sense wheels within wheels moving inside him, a churning depth of ponderings and musings beyond my comprehension, as if the wheels had been turning ages before I asked my question and would still be turning eons after my bones became dust.

The Woodsman moved away from the abyss, set his eyes, and focused on something behind me.

A rush of cold air hit. Shivering, I turned and followed his gaze.

Impossible! Why hadn't I seen it before? It was a great tree. It reminded me of a ponderosa pine, yet it was many times larger than a California redwood, perhaps sixty feet in diameter and

rising above the clouds. The reddish bark was rough, with splinters so jagged they looked like barbed fishhooks.

The tree cast a long shadow to the west, plunging into the chasm.

When I looked back at the Woodsman, he held a great sword with ancient inscriptions in a language I'd never seen. He walked to the tree, put a hand on it, and softly touched his head against it. Lifting the great sword and feeling its sharpness with his finger, he swung it back, uncoiling it against the trunk of the tree. The bark exploded, chunks flying everywhere.

I couldn't imagine how a tree this massive could be cut through—not by the greatest ax and certainly not with a sword.

What did he think he was doing?

EIGHT

I watched as the Woodsman swung the sword again and again with terrible force.

He paused once to take off his white outer robe and rewrap it around his midsection, leaving his dark chest bare. His sinewy muscles rippled as he hewed the wood. He thrashed and pounded, again and again. Sweat poured down his forehead and off his face. Small capillaries in his brow burst with the pressure, mingling blood with sweat.

I stepped close to the Woodsman, alarmed at his exertion and the toll it was taking on him. He spoke as he labored, and I listened, hearing things I'd never heard, things I'd never thought of—about himself, about me, about life.

"I offer a joy that will cost you everything you have but gain you everything that matters."

What did he mean?

"You've fallen short, and a terrible price must be paid."

I backed away, troubled. Was he saying I was at fault for all this? Was he siding with Shadrach, against me? How dare he accuse me? Why was I always being blamed?

I couldn't explain how any man could attack a tree with a diameter ten times larger than his height and continue, relentlessly, to swing a sword against it, causing his muscles to quiver with the shock of each impact. Nor could I explain why his sword didn't break or dull. But I saw it nonetheless with my own skeptic's eyes.

Finally I asked, "Can I help you?"

"No," he said, eyes lonesome. "You can't."

Did he think I had nothing to offer? Was I not good enough for him?

He chopped on that tree all day and through a long, lonely night. I dozed on and off, feeling useless but engrossed by what he was doing.

In the morning, with one final swing of his sword, the whole tree wobbled. The Woodsman stood motionless, staring at it. Time seemed to stand still, as if the entire cosmos had found its focal point, and whatever happened next would forever alter history itself.

He raised his right hand and pushed the tree toward the west. It tipped slowly and eerily before gravity seized it and began to slam it downward.

Mesmerized by the awesome sight, I felt relieved it wasn't going to crush me.

The great tree fell. And fell and fell, as if plunging a greater distance than could be imagined. I knew it was tall, disappearing above the clouds, but it dawned on me that to take that long to fall it must be far taller than I had imagined. I imagined it would make a lonely sight falling into the chasm. But finally it hit the ground with what seemed the force of a great warhead. The impact tossed me into the air. I landed facedown, sprawled on the ground.

But...why didn't the tree plummet into the chasm? It had landed crosswise. This could only mean...its top had reached the far edge! Impossible as it seemed, the great tree now bridged both sides of the abyss. The tree had been incomprehensibly long in its reach.

The Woodsman lay in a heap, sweating, exhausted, his biceps bulging, his veins throbbing, his worn clothes stained crimson.

He stood. He looked across the expanse to the other side of the chasm and walked to the base of the fallen tree. He slowly took off his sandals and set them on the ground.

Then I heard a creepy buzzing noise. I walked closer and looked down. At the Woodsman's feet I saw tiny people, the size of insects, maybe half an inch tall. I carefully got on my knees for a closer look. The little people scurried about and wrapped fragile threads around the Woodsman's feet. To people so small, the threads must have seemed like great ropes.

"We have him now," I heard one gloat. His voice sounded like it was intended to be somber and threatening, but it was

so high pitched that it was only a squeak. "He can't get away from us."

"He can't tell us what to do."

"We'll show him. We'll force him onto the tree!"

I heard squeak after squeak making similar threats, until I laughed and called down to them, "With one flick of a toe he would break your threads, and with a stomp of his feet he would smash you all!"

I ridiculed the pathetic, arrogant men below, but suddenly I stopped laughing when I found myself standing next to them. Eye to eye with them now, I saw a huge shadow and looked up. There, far above me, was...the Woodsman! Had I become small? Or had the Woodsman become big? Perhaps it was both. Maybe that explained how he had cut through the huge tree.

I was so much smaller than I'd thought, and he was so much bigger than he'd looked—things were not as they appeared.

I heard the sound of someone pounding with a hammer, but it was not the crisp, loud sound of nails driven into wood. Rather, it was a dull tearing sound. Where was it coming from?

I heard jingling metal and looked around to see people pulling things from their pockets. I reached into my left pocket and pulled out...a handful of nails.

I saw now that each person carried a hammer. I watched motionless as person after person positioned nails on the Woodsman's giant feet.

"No!" I shouted. "What has he done to you?"

What horrified me most was that the people seemed so normal, even nice. They weren't criminals. They appeared to be respected citizens.

"Beautiful day, isn't it?" a woman in green nurse's scrubs asked me as she positioned a nail and hammered it five times until it was buried to its head in the Woodsman's foot.

"Where's your hammer?" asked a businessman in suit and tie, a man who looked remarkably like my father and spoke like him too. "Here's an extra. A gift from me to you."

I took the hammer. It hung limp in my right hand.

After I had watched the others for a few minutes, what they were doing somehow seemed less appalling. Something moved in my chest, and before I knew it, I was thinking about how big the Woodsman was, and how distant he was, and how little he cared about me, and how he hadn't made my life go the way I wanted, and how he thought he was better than me, and how he'd cast blame on me, and how he refused my help in cutting the tree.

I lifted my hammer and started pounding nails into his heel. First one nail, then another and another. I felt gleeful, almost giddy.

All my life the Woodsman had gotten his way.

Now I would get mine.

NINE

I hammered nails feverishly, swinging my arm harder and harder, aching from the impact. Oddly, no matter how many nails I took out of my pocket, it remained full.

I thought about the Woodsman, how much this must be hurting him. The individual nails might have felt like a pinprick, but the cumulative effect of all those people, untold thousands, pounding all those nails, must have been agonizing.

I began to weep and threw down my hammer and tried to pull away. But I could only get so far—I realized now that I was tied to the others with the sticky strands of a great web, strong and binding, and I couldn't break loose. After picking my hammer back up, I did what everyone else was doing.

"He makes us suffer," someone said, pointing upward, then pounding another nail into his foot.

"Take that," I bellowed, and pounded nail after nail into his heel. I cursed him for everything that came to mind, including my sore arm, throbbing as if from blunt force trauma. But the

trauma was self-inflicted, you might be thinking. That was the furthest thing from my mind, which had been eclipsed by livid accusation and blinding blame.

"Look out!" someone yelled. People scattered, some of them pointing upward. A water droplet as big as a couch splashed on the ground, moisture flying everywhere. It felt warm on my face and had a salty taste.

"Back to work," someone shouted, and we moved close to his feet again, grabbing our nails and positioning our hammers as if going back to an assembly line after lunch hour.

For another stinging moment I grasped the horror of what I was doing. I wept.

But after wiping my eyes, I grew angry at how I'd suffered, how my dad wasn't there for me, and how my family had abandoned me and my boss hadn't chosen me to be vice president. I picked the hammer back up, pulled the replenished stock of nails out of my pocket, and started pounding again.

I couldn't remember the last time I'd thought of Charis or looked for it across the chasm. But at that moment, in the distance, out of the shining city of Charis rose a thunderous glow, an army of millions, first hovering over the city, then streaking through the sky like meteors. They flew across the chasm.

I expected the great army to settle upon the earth like a plague of locusts, devouring every living thing, myself among them. But once they arrived, above the Woodsman, they appeared unable to descend. I looked up to see that vast army of bright warriors suddenly break rank, then start beating down upon a transparent ceiling, or what was a ceiling from my vantage point, but would have been a floor to them. Swords unsheathed, they jammed themselves against a closed portal in the barrier. I heard their muffled pleas as they called to the Woodsman.

"Let us tend your wounds, World Maker."

"Let us grind your enemies into the dirt and raise your royal standards in their blood!"

"Let us fight the holy war now and bury the bent ones once and for all!"

They paced like caged lions, looking down, seeking permission, longing for a single word to unleash them. I shuddered at the sight of them, legion upon legion, crowding down, pressing and pushing, crying out and begging leave to destroy those who drove nails into the Woodsman's feet.

"Let us run the cowards through with the sword of your righteousness."

"Let us forever rid the cosmos of their evil."

The more we drove our nails down below, the more frantic became the warriors above. They pushed against the glass ceiling until I heard cracking and feared it would burst.

The Woodsman raised his hand to the warriors and sternly shook his head. His voice, ancient and deep and stern, called out, "Hold your place!"

It was then I felt something under my feet. I looked down to see the ground beneath me thin out and transform until it became a clear glass floor. Monstrous faces pressed their mouths and snouts against the glass, smearing it with drool and mucus.

I tried to step away from what I saw, but I couldn't escape them because they were everywhere below me. They were warriors like those in the sky above, yet very different—like a pack of rabid dogs compared to a kennel of healthy ones. But the contrast was far greater, as the beasts were a degenerate version of the noble warriors, different even in form now, all the more horrifying because I somehow knew they once had been like them.

I closed my eyes, hardly able to look, but when I opened them again, the twisted creatures were still there, pushing and pressing up.

Their eyes were cold gray, icy as death itself. They were bloodless, the eyes of predators, like those of the dark lord who had hunted me on the plain. In contrast, the eyes of the warriors above were hot and furious. I couldn't decide which terrified me more, the eyes of ice or the eyes of fire.

The shark-eyed warriors below kept pressing up against the floor, searching for every crack, just like their counterparts above. The ground beneath me pushed up, and my heart raced. Would these dark creatures escape from their pit? What would they do to us? Would it be worse than what the warriors above wanted to do to us?

When the warriors above reached a crescendo in their shouting and bludgeoning the barrier, the evil beasts stopped their carnage and looked far above. I saw fear in their eyes. I too feared the great army overhead, for it had become too clear whose side I was really on.

I realized in a moment of clarity that the world I'd always lived in, which I thought was the only world, was in fact a narrow isthmus caught between two great continents whose armies met here in battle. These forces clashing on the battleground of my world were powerful beyond measure and fought so desperately that the stakes must be higher than I could comprehend.

The Woodsman looked down and cleared his throat. The warriors shuddered, winced, and backed away from the glass, covering their hideous faces as if anticipating a decree of doom.

I held my breath. What would he say? Would he end it all now? Would I disintegrate in the conflagration of his judgment?

At last the Woodsman's face slightly relaxed. Slowly and sadly he nodded at the beasts below. "Yes," he whispered, a whisper that blew a powerful wind, forcing me to my knees.

The faces of the beasts lit with malevolent glee. They swarmed beneath me in a circle, like a black tornado. The land quaked, the glass floor cracked open, and foul-smelling gases erupted.

Ten yards from me, right at the Woodsman's feet, the glass shattered. An army of flying beasts screeched and squawked and cackled, celebrating their release like drunken pirates.

Some of the creatures flew near to us. "Don't let him push you around," one of them cried in shrill but perfectly enunciated words that chilled me.

"You can do whatever you want," another one told us. "He's not your master." Some of the reptiles whispered suggestions; some screamed commands into the ears of the little people pounding their nails into the Woodsman's heel. The beasts herded in more and more of us, close to his bleeding feet.

In one moment I felt outraged at the people piercing him with nails, and in the next I looked down to see myself positioned on the Woodsman's foot, my own hand bringing down hammer on nail—again and again and again.

Winged dinosaurs hovered over us, trying to sink their claws into the Woodsman. The flying beasts looked huge to us, but they were small enough that the Woodsman easily could have swatted or squashed them. Several of them pecked at the center of his hands, drawing blood, the droplets falling to the ground with a huge splash. Still the beasts seemed limited in their ability to harm the Woodsman directly. Strangely, they had their greatest success convincing the little people to do their dirty work.

"The tyrant is your enemy," one of them shouted. "He has no right to mistreat you like he does!" The monster swooped low, pushing aside me and several others. I rolled, then arose, shoving and kicking the people who struck and screamed at me. I hated them for trying to inflict their will on me. Seething with rage, I pulled more nails from my pocket and held them in my mouth. Intending to inflict them on these horrid little people, in rapid succession I ended up driving them into the Woodsman's heel instead, drawing his blood.

"Take that!" I shouted. "No one can tell me how to run my life. How dare you treat me like this?"

The great foot trembled, as if in a spasm, but did not move away from me. For a fleeting moment I wondered why I was punishing the Woodsman for what the beast had done, for what I had done, and for what the little people had done to me. But in the next moment, it all seemed to make perfect sense. He was to blame for everything.

It felt so good to be in control, to determine my own destiny, to be the master of my fate. I was choosing to do something with my hands, something that made a difference. I was in charge; the Woodsman was at my mercy—and I showed him none. Why should I? What had he ever done for me?

Another great drop of salt water fell from above, hitting the bleeding foot and splashing on me, stinging my eyes. I cursed, wiped my eyes, and blinked hard. I grabbed another nail and started pounding, making up for lost time, drawing more blood.

The more I swung the hammer, the more automatic and easier it became. Blood of the innocent, shed at my whim and convenience? *It's not the first time,* I thought, then immediately pushed back nagging memories to the dark corners of my mind. No—what I'd done twenty years ago and what I was doing now was reasonable and just. And besides, everyone else was doing it.

With so many others doing the same thing, it couldn't be bad, could it?

I heard voices far above and stopped hammering long enough to look. I saw in the sky, just below the Woodsman's face, the commander of the army of light, the same mighty one I'd seen on the battlefield who had appeared to come to my rescue before abruptly stopping. Apparently he alone had been permitted to pass down through the glass ceiling.

Walking on the air as if it were concrete, he bowed his knees and, eyes pleading, looked at the Woodsman. It seemed inconceivable that this great warrior would take orders from anyone. His bowed knees indicated that he considered the Woodsman his commander-in-chief. An unlikely notion, but inescapable.

The Woodsman, his head four times taller than the warrior's body, returned the gaze of his general, then for a moment hung his head and winced. He shifted on his feet. A guttural groan surfaced from within him, like distant thunder.

The general, still on one knee, spoke. "Let us destroy them now, Master." His deep voice, like a bass reverb of 200 decibels, shook air above and the ground beneath me. *"Please,"* he said, so loud and emphatic that my nerve endings exploded in response.

"Michael," replied the Woodsman in a tired, heavy voice, "if that was what I wanted, you know I could unmake them all in a single moment. I could destroy them with a word...or merely a thought."

"But why, Master, do you not let us protect you and defend your honor? *Why* do you let them torture you?"

The Woodsman's wet eyes drooped. He paused long before answering. Finally he said, "Because it's the only way I can save them."

The warrior-lord searched the air for more words. Finding none, at last he bowed his head, rose, and backed away, continuing to look downward as if he could not bear to see his Lord's tortured eyes.

As their general passed up through the glass, the soldiers of light listened in rapt attention to his report. I heard some of them groan and shout, while others stood in stunned silence. Again they brought swords down on the invisible barrier, some of them beating upon it with their great clenched fists. For a moment I thought they would surely break through. I clenched my teeth, knowing if they escaped, my comrades and I would be crushed in an instant by the cosmic weight of their wrath.

They pushed and swung their mighty swords downward until at last the ceiling cracked. I cringed and braced myself.

"Noooooo!"

Everything shook at the lionlike roar. At the utterance of the Woodsman's word, millions of warriors froze, then were sucked up into invisible regions of the sky as if into the vacuum of space. They disappeared, all of them, even their general. Gone.

Above the clouds, there was nothing but silence.

The Woodsman stood alone.

From under the ground and on the earth shouts of gleeful malice erupted. The beasts ran wild, serial killers with the restraint of law enforcement removed. They swooped and bit at the Woodsman's neck, while prodding the little people below to keep piercing his heel, from which blood gushed.

I looked at the blood on my own hands. I gazed up at the giant Woodsman, certain that in one moment, deliberate or unguarded, he could hurl us all into the chasm.

Something grabbed hold of my insides and made me stop and wonder. I looked up at him, holding out my bloody hands, hammer and nails in them, and cried out to him, "Why do you do what you do?"

He looked down at me, into my eyes, as if I were the only one there. "*You* are why I do what I do."

My heart felt drawn toward him. Then I considered his words. Was he blaming me again? How dare he? I backed away. He stretched down his bloody hand, palm open, and I retreated farther. It nearly touched me. Chest quaking, in self-defense I pulled from my pocket a nail. Feverishly, I pounded it into the center of his hand.

A great dark cloud formed and spread. The sky looked as if it had been rubbed hard by a dirty eraser. Within seconds a ferocious wind blew, lightning struck, and thunder roared.

The Woodsman stood alone at the base of the tree. I couldn't see the nails in his feet now. He climbed up the side of the fallen tree, slowly and deliberately, cutting hands and feet on the barbs in the bark. Reaching the top, he stood and walked, his right foot bleeding profusely, especially from the deepest wounds in his heel. The fishhook spurs of the great tree cut into his feet, but he kept walking and wincing, walking and wincing.

He seemed so terribly alone.

The hell hawks circled over him. The farther he walked on the tree the darker it became.

When he was only barely visible, I saw him stop, raise his hands, and lie down on the tree. He disappeared into the darkness. I couldn't tell where he ended and the darkness began; he had become inseparable from it.

For an eternal moment there was nothing, as if all creation braced itself. Then I heard a terrible thud—one, then another, and another, as if hands and instruments from a different world fell down on the tree. The force of blows from those great hands must have been much harder to bear than that of us little people.

I heard sounds like a flapping tarp, then morbid victory shrieks. Then soft weeping. Then nothing.

There was a long silence in which I stared out into the darkness of the tree, the darkness of the chasm, and the darkness within me, unable to distinguish one from the others. Then at last, as if a great lion had been pierced with an arrow, the air filled with a solitary roar.

"Whyyyyyy?"

The Woodsman's voice seemed to come not just from the fallen tree lying across the chasm, but from the depths of the abyss itself. It shook the earth beneath me and the heavens above.

The gray sky of death descended on the fallen tree.

The longer I looked into the darkness, the more I could see. Despite the distance, I beheld the Woodsman pinned to the tree like an insect to a collector's board.

Above him I saw the great shark-eyed flying reptile, the prince of beasts, surrounded by his flailing minions. They circled as if riding a column of air. Wings outspread, the beast-prince descended upon the tree, approaching his prey cautiously. He first tested the Woodsman with a single claw, then two claws. I heard his deep-throated gurgle of delight as the Woodsman offered no resistance. He clamped his needle-sharp teeth on him, then lashed at him with his claws, becoming bolder and bolder.

A guttural voice cried out from the beast, dripping darkness, a voice like but disturbingly unlike that of the great warrior Michael.

"*Bleed, Holy One!* Suffer and die, Prince of fools!"

His foul claws clutching the Woodsman's neck, the flying reptile dug into the Woodsman's eyes. Suddenly the smaller beasts pounced like jackals, picking and eating and gorging themselves on the morbid feast that was the Woodsman's body.

I turned away, crying out at the horror of it. The complete injustice. I wept partly for the Woodsman's agony, partly for my complicity in it. For though that great beast frightened and repulsed me, though it had wanted to kill me and would have if not stopped by an invisible hand, the truth fell upon me like a stony avalanche. I had become the beast's partner in the murder of the Woodsman. I myself, Nick Seagrave, had pounded nails in his flesh.

Pacing now, I told myself that the nails I'd pounded weren't fatal, that really they were little more than pinpricks in the Woodsman's feet. But the wetness I'd seen in the Woodsman's eyes, the saltwater tears and the gut-wrenching tone of his voice said otherwise.

How could I be part of something so monstrous? I'd always believed I was a decent person — sincere, well-motivated, that my good outweighed my bad. If it came to it, I would be good enough to make the grade.

Then, in a flood of doubt, I asked myself: Who was this man whose face I'd seen every day in the mirror, who swung the hammer, who chose to inflict suffering? Who was this Nick Seagrave who had sided with the beast? Why did I hate the Woodsman so much that I would hurt him so badly? And why, a moment later, did part of me desperately want to love him, so much that I felt I would die if I could not?

I lay on hard, unforgiving ground, my body aching, my soul tortured by my questions, assaulted by my guilt.

Believing the Woodsman was dead already, I was surprised to hear three final words shouted from the center of the tree over the chasm: "Paid in Full!"

The Woodsman's words shook the mountains, from the rising of the sun to its setting. The rocks split; the earth to the far east folded over itself like an ocean wave, molten rock erupting. But what did the words mean?

I heard the rip of fabric, as if the cosmos were a great cloak torn down the center. The sound started far above the sky and hit the ground with a violent tremor. After that, nothing.

In the far distance, the silence of Charis seemed deafening. Had the city's occupants all been sucked away with the warriors above? Had the planet been left in the hands of demon-beasts?

Below my feet I heard sounds of glee, the cruel celebration of the bloodless. At last I heard sounds from above and from the west, sounds of weeping.

The City of Darkness rejoiced. The City of Light mourned. Babel partied while Charis wailed in despair.

Through low dark clouds I watched the Woodsman lying

there, lifeless, on the tree. Something dripped into the great chasm. And though the drops were small, I could hear them land a million miles below. Their echoes filled the canyon and reverberated inside my skull.

The King was dead.

And I had killed him.

ELEVEN

My whole body was covered with dirt and blood that had formed into a red clay. Numb, I stumbled around until I found a pumice stone and a small puddle of dirty, undrinkable water. I tried to wash the bloodstains from my hands. I couldn't. The more I scrubbed, the more the dirt and blood spread.

I grabbed fistfuls of nails from my pocket, again and again, throwing them on the ground or over into the chasm. But still there were more.

How could I avoid blame for shedding the Woodsman's blood? I'd hammered the nails, hadn't I? I'd stung his feet as surely as if I were a scorpion or one of the twisted beasts.

Still, why hadn't he been willing to listen to me, to do what I wanted, to use his power to help me fulfill my goals instead of thwarting them? He was asking for it—his death was as much his fault as mine. No, it was *more* his fault. He hadn't even let me help him cut down the tree!

Had I really hammered those nails? Or was it my imagination, fueled by those wretched guilt feelings? I was being too hard on myself. Even if I'd driven the nails, I wouldn't have done it without a good reason, would I? Self-defense—that was it. I was no killer. I wasn't perfect, but I was a decent person, better than most men.

Back and forth I wavered, one minute wallowing in grief and guilt, the next in anger and denial and self-defense.

In the distance, over the chasm, I heard the predators continue their feeding frenzy, ravaging the Woodsman's carcass.

Did I really help serve them up this gruesome meal?

I paced, kicking rocks, spitting out dust. I moved near the edge of the chasm and gazed at it again, thinking maybe somehow it would look different this time.

It didn't.

Suddenly I heard the tortured howl of a beast. I looked up to see the great winged reptile, the dark lord, retreating from the tree. The howl was quickly followed by hundreds of shrieks from the circling minions.

Aaack! Aaack! The piercing airy sounds shook me to the core.

The lesser reptiles flew toward our side of the chasm, fleeing in chaos from whatever it was they saw. Circling wildly, crashing into one another, they spied the hole in the glass floor and spiraled downward, crowding through and disappearing.

A booming sound, like an approaching freight train, came from the center of the tree. A gigantic stone was rolling on top of the tree with enormous momentum, headed my way. If it reached my side of the chasm, it would surely crush me.

As the flying beast-prince tried to flee, it was yanked down by an invisible force, and its head lay on the horizontal tree. It squawked dreadfully as the great stone rolled over it, crushing its head.

Somehow the beast managed to flail its way toward the edge of the chasm, head mangled and bleeding. It wove through the air, thrashing and falling. It skidded to the ground no more than fifty feet from me. Then it got up, staggering, as if evil itself were fighting off death. Its cold murky eyes stared at me, freezing my blood. I felt sure its wound was fatal, but the beast uttered a grisly cry, then wobbled to the hole in the ground and disappeared in a swirl, as if sucked down a drain.

The stone, still rolling, flew off the end of the tree, coming so near to me I had to leap out of its way. Behind it walked a solitary figure—the Woodsman, wearing his white robe, now unstained by blood or sweat or tears.

Then the whole world shifted before me. The land I stood on seemed to sink, and the land on the other side of the chasm rose—and Charis with it.

The tree was no longer horizontal but vertical, still connecting the two worlds, no longer as bridge but as ladder. Against the

upright tree stood the Woodsman himself, though somehow he was much bigger than the tree. His feet touched the ground of the lower world, and his head rose above the ground of the upper world. He held the tree in his hand, and it seemed to transform from an instrument of death to a means of life.

The cosmos had been reoriented. For a moment, the upside down became right side up.

No sooner had this happened than everything became just like before, horizontal again — two worlds joined by one bridge, the great tree, and the Woodsman once more the size of a man.

Throughout my education and upbringing, the retaining walls of my mind had been carefully constructed to deny the supernatural, to explain away the miraculous. Now they fell to the ground like flimsy shacks in a hurricane.

I knew, in the face of the Woodsman's return from the abyss and his reentry into the world of the living, that the course of my journey had been charted by an unseen hand, which had led me not just to this world but to this moment.

I felt awe. But also terror.

I watched the Woodsman approach a young woman, gaunt and dirty and wounded. Wait, I knew her. It was Malaiki. I had seen her on the red road. She and the Woodsman were too far away for me to hear.

Eventually they moved toward the tree. They climbed up and walked upon it. Malaiki seemed to buckle and falter, as if in pain. I feared she would fall. But now it became hard to see them—perhaps it was the sweat in my eyes. I could see only one blended form now, and soon it moved out of sight.

Despite the distance, it wasn't long before the Woodsman came back, without Malaiki. I felt envy and resentment. Why had he taken her and not me? Next he chose a man, handsome and young, who hung his head and bit his nails while they talked. What was going through his mind? Did he have the same doubts and fears as I? What was the Woodsman telling him? If only I could hear.

Eventually he, too, walked with the Woodsman to the tree. I thought I saw the young man shake, and I heard him cry out as he stepped onto it. Was the Woodsman pushing him? Forcing him? Or just holding him up?

The two of them walked the tree until they finally disappeared into the western sky.

Why had the Woodsman come for others before coming for me? Would he come for me at all? And what would I do if he didn't?

I'd do what I'd always done. I'd take care of myself. Besides, once they were out of my sight, the others likely fell to their death. One false move on that long walk and they'd plunge into the abyss. Perhaps they'd been shoved off. Yes, the Woodsman might have taken them away only to punish them for torturing him with the nails. This very moment they might be falling headlong into that bottomless pit.

I won't let that happen to me.

Now the Woodsman returned again—was he coming for me?

No, he went to another. But she didn't walk with him to the tree. Instead, after just a few minutes of conversation with him, she turned around and ambled away from the chasm.

I noticed many others walking away as well. They had found the chasm unsettling and upsetting. They were returning to the dead-end roads, preferring their empty fantasies to this bloody reality. A few of them joined the woman, giving her company on the road going back.

She hadn't gone more than thirty feet when she stopped to look back at the Woodsman, then turned and kept walking farther. A hundred feet away, she glanced back again, then once more at perhaps three times that distance. When one of her companions tugged on her arm, she departed for good, turning her back to the chasm and to the Woodsman.

I watched, almost hypnotized by her departure as she disappeared on the plain.

I could run and catch her within ten minutes.

I took several steps in her direction. But what would I tell her when I caught her? Would I try to bring her back here? Or would I go away with her, as far away from this place as I could? Part of me answered one way, part the other. I didn't know which part I should listen to.

When at last I looked back toward the chasm, I saw someone else walking the tree with the Woodsman. An older man, he appeared to slip and fall. My heart stopped, until the crosser of the chasm pulled him up again. They disappeared, and I couldn't see what was happening.

Would the Woodsman come back for me?

Did I want him to?

TWELVE

After a long wait, I raised my eyes from the powdered bone and dust. The Woodsman was returning, taking long, deliberate strides atop the fallen tree. I felt my heart in my throat.

He was headed right for me.

Though he was unmistakably a man, even at a distance I could see his eyes, wild and uncontrollable, the eyes of a lion. Not a lion who would be tamed, but a fierce king with jaws that could devour me at any moment.

As he came near, I stared into those eyes, deep and dark. He looked at me through lenses far bigger than a man's. Those eyes were doorways to another world. He saw every inch of me, outside and in. That made me squirm.

I looked down at his hands and feet and shuddered at the scars I saw there. I examined my bloodstained hands and stared at the ground, utterly ashamed.

He spoke my name.

I said nothing and didn't look up.

"The deed is done," he announced. "The price is paid. The red road continues now. I have made it so. The tree is there to cross. Now at last, as image-bearers have feared to dream, there is a way to Charis, the City of Light. Will you accept my invitation to cross the chasm?"

"But how *can* it be crossed? It's so huge."

"The chasm is huge, but the tree is bigger still. And I am far bigger even than the tree."

I asked him about the others who'd gone before me. "Did they make it to the far side? Or did they...fall off and die?"

"They did not fall off. But in a sense they did die."

What? My stomach tightened.

"You cannot cross the chasm without dying. But if you stay here, you will also die. If you walk the tree, you will die in a different way. But the tree is the only way to life. In one way, you're already dead, though you've continued to exist. You may choose to die and stay dead, or you may die and embrace life—but in either case you must die. Nothing that has not died can be raised from the dead."

"I don't understand."

"You don't have to understand. But in order to cross the chasm, you have to trust me."

"I'll do what I can, but...I'm not sure it will be enough."

"I am sure what you can do will *never* be enough." He said it with kindness in his eyes, yet it hit me like an insult. "You cannot earn your way, Nick. You must give up on that idea. You may receive the gift of passage I freely offer, the gift I purchased. Admit your responsibility for the abyss. Acknowledge that you pierced my skin with your nails. Affirm that I am the World Shaper who crossed the chasm for you. Ask me to deliver you from all that torments you. And invite me to walk you across the chasm."

Objections descended on me like a swarm of flies. I felt a terrible sting within. I remembered Joshua telling me, "Be careful whom you trust." Could I really trust the Woodsman? Maybe he wasn't who he appeared to be. Maybe he only wanted to get me over the chasm so he could push me off the tree.

"I'm not sure," I said. "I don't think I'm ready."

"I've done what was necessary. I've made my choice—now you must make yours."

I balked at that, hungering to have more certainty before making any decision. I looked at him, shrugging my shoulders. "Just…who are you?" I asked.

"I am the Source of your life and of your dreams. I am what you dream of when your dreams are good. But be warned—to those who do not embrace the good dream, I become the nightmare."

I shivered at the tone of his voice.

"You've only now begun to see me clearly—and there's much about me you still don't see. Do you have something to say to me?"

I stayed quiet for several minutes. Then I swallowed hard, both eager to talk and dreading it.

"I used to be so sure of myself," I began, "certain I wasn't to blame, that whatever went wrong was someone else's fault. I blamed my wife, my children, my father, my co-workers, the church, the neighbors. And maybe...*you,* though I didn't know it was you."

He stared at me, attentive but silent, refusing to let me off the hook by speaking.

I choked a bit. "I feel like all my life I've been wrapped up in nothing but myself, full of self-deception and self-pity and self-preoccupation."

The Woodsman looked at me, nodding. He waited, as if I must say more.

I obliged, rehearsing to him every offense, every failing, everything I could think of—everything from pride and arrogance to lust and greed and the failure to be the man my wife and children needed. It took a long time, because the more I said, the more my eyes were opened to what I'd never seen before. Each confession led to the next, like a mile of dominoes falling on each other.

Finally I said, "That's all I can think of for now. But there must be many other wrongs I've done."

"Yes," he said. "In time I'll show them to you so at last you may be free of them."

I shuddered, wondering what he was thinking of. But as I gazed into his eyes, his words gave me comfort. A wild river of peace I hadn't known since childhood, if even then, flooded my barren insides and lapped at its dusty banks. My craggy heart, for a moment at least, stopped aching and became soft to the Woodsman's touch.

Quietly he took my hand, and we walked to the tree. I looked down at the abyss and felt my face twitch. Sweat dripped from my forehead to my cheeks.

"What if I fall?" I asked him.

I expected to hear reassurance, but he said nothing. With his help I stepped onto the tree, which was red with blood. My feet were cut immediately, and I began to bleed. I walked only ten yards before my feet were bloody pulps, and I could go no farther.

I looked at him, not knowing what to do—knowing only that I wanted to cross the chasm but could not.

The Woodsman picked me up and held me in his arms. For a fleeting moment I remembered my father holding me like this when he carried me into the emergency room after my bike accident on my tenth birthday.

The Woodsman walked on, picking up the pace. If he made one false step, I'd fall into the abyss. For an instant I wished I'd stayed on the safe ground of the chasm's edge.

Safe? I questioned myself. How much worse could *anything* be than lying abandoned on the rim of the abyss?

If the Woodsman couldn't do what he claimed, I was lost. But, I told myself, *if he can't do what he claims, all is lost anyway.*

As we crossed the chasm, he stopped near the middle. His great scarred hands wiped the dirt and blood off me and onto himself. The dirtier the Woodsman became, the cleaner I became, until he was completely dirty and I was completely clean.

I looked down into the abyss and shivered at the spiraling darkness below, a drain that seemed to suck ever downward. He drew me close to his chest, and I felt secure in his strong arms. What place could be safer? I gazed into those wide brown eyes and felt I was seeing him, and all the universe itself, for the first time.

As we approached the far edge of the chasm, I knew something deep inside me, something remarkable, paradoxical, even impossible: though it was still me, I knew without a doubt that I was not the same person who'd stepped out onto the tree.

As we came to the end of the tree I pointed toward Charis, more beautiful than ever, a Paradise of laughter and joy. For the first time I was close enough to see trees and flowers and waterfalls, a great river and animals bounding near its banks. It was so much closer than before, almost within reach. The Woodsman smiled as he saw my delight. Seemingly he found joy in my joy, or was it that I found joy in his?

On the chasm's other side, the Woodsman leapt off the tree with me still in his arms, cushioning me from the impact. When he put my feet on the ground, I looked at the new terrain, lush with vegetation. I looked back at the abyss and gazed wide-eyed at how far we'd come.

I stared down into the chasm. Was I imagining this? How could we have crossed something so immense in what had seemed only a few minutes?

The Woodsman put his hand on my shoulder. I turned and saw up close the terrible gash in his flesh. Looking at his eyes, I didn't know if I was seeing his tears or mine. Or both.

"I did it for you," he told me.

I wasn't sure what to say.

"I would have done it for you alone."

I hung my head, feeling both unworthiness and awe.

"And if there was need, I would do it for you again."

I looked at him and could only wonder why.

"But there is no need to ever do it again. It is finished. Paid in full."

I reached down to my left pocket. I gasped as I felt the bulge. One by one I pulled out the shafts of pointed metal. On them I saw dried blood. How could this be?

"I still have nails in my pocket."

"Yes. But only for now. There will be none in Charis."

I looked at him with surprise. Weren't we about to enter Charis?

"I don't deserve what you've done for me," I said.

"Of course you don't." He smiled. "If you deserved it, you wouldn't need it. And I wouldn't have had to die to give it to you."

"But if you knew all I've done, all that's inside me..."

"*If?* Do you still not understand? I know everything. I'm never taken by surprise. There are no skeletons in your closet. I took care of them all. You were wrong—I don't expect the impossible of you. But I've done the impossible *for* you."

He reached out his hands to me, hands I once would have thought monstrous. I held them, putting my fingers on his scars. I lowered my forehead to his marred hands.

When I looked up, I gazed at Charis, poised beautifully on a mountain, appearing more distant than just a minute before, though reachable now, the red road winding toward it. But why did it still seem far away?

"I'm confused," I said to the Chasm Crosser. "We're not there yet."

"No. Your journey isn't over. Your service for me is just beginning. There was no work you could do for me on the other side of the chasm. But I have much work for you to do on this side."

"And when the work is done?"

"Then you'll enter Charis, capital city of my unending country that stretches to the far reaches of this world and all worlds. And should you ever make it to the end, I'll create new worlds for you that surpass anything you've ever imagined."

I felt my ears move back, pushed by my grin. But I wondered whether my smile could be as big as his.

"I don't want to wait. I long to go to Charis now."

"Why?" he asked, surprising me.

"To escape from reality—maybe that's part of it."

He laughed. "Going to Charis is not escaping reality—it's entering reality! You've always lived in the Shadowlands. Yet in your dreams I've given you glimpses of the City of Light. That's why Charis has always called to you. That's why you've always longed for it—even when you walked the roads that robbed you of joy and hope."

"But why is it still far away?" I asked, pointing to the west.

"At moments Charis will seem close to you; sometimes it will seem impossibly far. But as you walk the red road, at every day's end you'll be one day closer to Charis. One day closer to me, One day closer to home."

"Home?"

"Yes. The world you were made for. The world I am making for you."

"Will I miss life on earth?"

He looked at me oddly. "You will live forever on the earth! A transformed earth, where I will put my throne, where I will forever dwell with my people. You will have a new body—your old body made new. You will have a new mind—your old mind made new. You will live on a new earth—the old earth made new. I don't give up, you know. I didn't give up on the earth, and I didn't give up on you. I came not to destroy but to redeem my fallen creation."

"I won't have to give up the things I love about this world?"

"On the contrary, all that is good in this world will be part of the world to come. What will be forever gone are death and evil and suffering and the dark lord and his beasts. The best is yet to come. My children never pass their peak in this earth. They will at last reach their peak on the new earth." He smiled broadly. "You will, as the storytellers say, all live happily ever after."

"Will you stay with me until then?"

"I'm going ahead. I'll be there to welcome you when you arrive."

My heart sang and sank in the same moment.

"You're leaving me then?"

"Not really. I'll be inside." He put his hand on my chest. "And I'll be around you, even when you can't see me. Don't imagine I've left. I will never leave you, never forsake you. *Never.*"

"How will I know the way?"

He handed me a big book with an old, worn cover. "This is my guidebook. Its stories, words of wisdom and truth, will show you the way. You must read it daily and ponder its words and ask my help to obey them."

"But even with the book...how will I survive the dangers of the road? How will I keep from turning around or dying on the way?"

"You must no longer travel alone."

"But...who will I travel with?"

"My followers. You have met some of them. You must walk with them and help each other believe and understand and follow my book. You must remind each other of my promises, speaking *of* me and talking *to* me."

"But some of your followers are...well, difficult."

"Yes," he said. "Nearly as difficult as you are." He smiled. "But it is nonetheless essential that you walk the road together and treat each other as I have treated you. How you relate to each other is of utmost importance to me."

"But these people aren't easy to get along with."

"And you are? Don't fall back into the arrogance you've just confessed. You need each other all the more because you're so flawed. The enemy will do all he can to set you at each other's throats."

"The enemy. You mean Joshua?" I asked, hanging my head.

"Yes, he uses my name, rarely appearing or sounding as he really is. He is the usurper, the imposter. The beast who comes to kill and destroy and can disguise himself as a friend and mentor, a teacher of love and tolerance and positive affirmation. He will look for ways to get you to devour each other. If he can separate you from other road walkers, he'll defeat you. Without each other, you cannot survive."

"The place you said you're building for us...what will it be like?"

"A home perfectly suited to you." He smiled. "You'll like it. I'm not only a woodsman, I'm a carpenter. I make things and I fix things. I made the universe. And soon I am going to fix it."

He drew me to himself in a strong embrace. I knew that he loved me, but in that moment I sensed something else...he *liked* me. We had become friends, and the friendship would grow forever. I would never exhaust his wealth or depth because there was no end to either.

Pondering that miracle of grace, I held on to him. I locked into the hug. I didn't blink, didn't move, didn't speak for fear of ending the moment. It was the moment for which I was made. I was embracing the truth I sought, the meaning I desired, the home I'd always yearned for.

Suddenly I felt a tightening of the hug, then a relaxing.

He was gone. Or rather, I could no longer *see* him.

But through a portal in the air, I saw a gathering on the other side. I knew it was Charis, the city on the hill far away, but so close now I could smell its delicious aromas and taste them on my tongue.

Hundreds of people were dressed in party garb, while dozens of great warriors served them delicacies. It was a great celebration.

Suddenly the Woodsman, in his white robe, joined them, smiling. I heard applause and laughter and saw toasts and festivity, rejoicing. I assumed the cause for their revelry was the return of their King.

But the Woodsman gestured my way, and I realized suddenly they were all looking at me. I appeared to be the topic of discussion. I saw glasses raised and strong arms held up on my behalf. They were cheering me on.

The portal closed, and they disappeared.

But though I couldn't see or hear it, I knew the party continued. *My* party—*I* was the cause for celebration!

The Chasm Crosser had come to me…so that I could come to him. And having come to each other, we could never be parted.

I turned and looked around me. There were people, many of them, of all shapes and sizes and colors and languages and personalities and temperaments. They, too, had been carried across the chasm in the Woodsman's arms. They, too, were looking toward Charis. They were gathering in groups to walk the red road together. In one of the groups stood the craggy-faced old man. He smiled at me with his missing tooth. Part of me wanted to look away, but I smiled too, because mostly I was glad to see him.

"Call me Shad," he said.

"Call me Nick," I said, extending my hand and touching him for the first time. "Nick Seagrave."

I decided to join Shad and his group of travelers, Malaiki among them. The Chasm Crosser had said I needed them. If I trusted him to carry me across the chasm, I must trust him in this also.

And perhaps I could help others to find the person they were made for—the Woodsman. And the place they were made for—Charis.

Perhaps I could lend them a hand, setting them on the road to my King…the road to Charis, my home.

+==+

＋══＋

Nick Seagrave's full story—all that happened before
and after he came to the Chasm—is told in the novel
Edge of Eternity.

READERS GUIDE

After reading each chapter in *The Chasm,* explore the corresponding set of questions below. In each chapter, be sure to look at Mike Biegel's art and ask yourself what important aspect of the story it captures.

Chapter 1

1. Nick Seagrave says the sight of the chasm was "devastating." What would you say is the central meaning of the chasm? What forms has the chasm taken in your life?

2. Is there something that draws you toward Heaven (and drew you even before you knew God), in the same way that the main character was drawn to Charis?

3. Why do you think Nick's first impression of Charis (seen from a distance) was so negative?

4. In what ways are his initial perceptions of the "dreadful tyrant" he sensed in Charis similar to the perceptions people have of God?

5. How trustworthy have your own first impressions of people and places been?

6. Charis is described as a place of light, music, pleasure, adventure, and celebration. In your experience, what place or

places have served as a foretaste of Heaven or of life on
the New Earth? (*Charis* is the Greek word for grace. The
author named Heaven in honor of God's grace, which is
what allows us entry to Heaven.)

7. In what ways is the character of Joshua admirable and
   appealing?

8. Nick liked the sense of control he was given by Joshua, his
   guide. Is your personality one that likes to feel in control?
   In what ways is that true for you?

9. What are the most significant things you learn about Nick
   when Joshua takes him to what appears to be Nick's
   office?

10. What things do you learn about Nick while he's in his
    condo?

11. What do you learn about Nick in the mall interiors and in
    the restaurant?

12. From what you've seen of Nick so far, in what ways are you
    and he alike? In what ways are you different?

Chapter 2

1. What, if anything, does Nick gain by giving in to his physi-
   cal lust and passions? What does he lose?

2. What's the apparent state of his relationship with his wife
   and with his children?

3. Nick says he came to see that "there's no such thing as a
   private moment; the whole cosmos is our audience for

everything we do in the dark." To what extent do you believe this statement is true?

4. Why do you think Nick is so certain that his children will go on "to choose their own wrong roads"?

5. Nick wonders: *If there is a hell, was I there already?* What's the best answer to that question?

6. Do you agree with Joshua's assessment of the "roads of religion and spirituality"—that "they all have something that will benefit you"? Why or why not?

7. Nick wonders if there is "such a thing as truth." What do you think?

8. What seems to be the significance of this battle that rages on the plain? What is Nick meant to learn from it?

Chapter 3

1. Who do you think these two opposing commanders in this battle are meant to represent? How literally do you think we should conceive of them?

2. Why do you think Nick is such an important target for the dark commander's hatred?

3. Nick contrasts his own life environment—one of "compromise, rule bending, trade-offs, concessions, bargaining, striking deals, finding middle ground"—with the sharp distinctions he perceives on the battlefield: "Good was good; evil was evil," and they shared no common ground. Which description matches best with your own view of life?

4. In our own lives and existence, is there an unseen supernatural war going on? If so, what do you know about it?
What signs do you see of it? What questions do you have
about it?

Chapter 4

1. What appear to be the major personality traits of the black-
robed character Nick observes in this chapter?
2. Who is this black-robed figure meant to represent?
3. What is most remarkable about the character Joshua?
4. Has there been anyone like Joshua in your own experience?
If so, who?

Chapter 5

1. Why had Nick been so reluctant earlier to listen to the rag-
gedly dressed white-haired man? Have you ever found it
hard to listen to people you find unappealing?
2. Nick notices the "trancelike movements" of people on the
gray roads, and the old man portrays them as misguided
and hopeless. How close does this describe people today?
3. What strikes you about the artwork in this chapter?
4. Nick asks the old man, "Why the great battle? And why is
evil winning?" As those questions relate to our own world
today, what do you think are the best answers? Or are they
unanswerable for the time being?

5. What is "walking the red road" about? Is Nick's choice to walk this road similar to any decision you've made? Why do you suppose the author chose for the road to be red?

Chapter 6

1. In the description given here of the chasm (or depicted in the artwork), as Nick encounters it up close, what elements stand out most to you?
2. Should we recognize anything like the chasm in our own lives? What is it meant to represent?
3. What is our own degree of responsibility for the chasm that separates us, or once separated us, from what is on the other side?
4. Why does Nick fall into such despair? In his mind and heart, what forces are at work? And how similar are they to forces at work in your own mind and heart?
5. Who or what do you believe the old man, Shadrach, represents?

Chapter 7

1. What stands out most to you in this chapter's description of the Woodsman?
2. Who is the Woodsman meant to represent?
3. What is the giant tree meant to represent? And why do you think the Woodsman is cutting the tree?

Chapter 8

1. Why won't the Woodsman allow Nick to help him cut down the tree? Why does Nick resent him for not receiving his help?

2. What is significant about the extensive and difficult labor required for the Woodsman to bring down the tree?

3. What do you think the nails are meant to represent?

4. What are the most important things Nick learns in this chapter?

Chapter 9

1. Nick experiences great swings in his attitudes toward the Woodsman and toward his own actions. To what degree is this similar to anything in your own life or that you've seen in others?

2. What is Nick meant to realize about the two armies—those above a glass ceiling, the others below a glass floor?

3. Nick says, "I realized in a moment of clarity that the world I'd always lived in, which I thought was the only world, was in fact a narrow isthmus caught between two great continents whose armies met here in battle. These forces clashing on the battleground of my world were powerful beyond measure and fought so desperately that the stakes must be higher than I could comprehend." Do you think this is an accurate description of our world? Why or why not?

4. To what degree do you think human beings have been accomplices with forces of supernatural evil in opposing what is supernaturally good?

Chapter 10

1. What are the most significant things Nick is learning in this chapter about the Woodsman?
2. Why do you think the Woodsman accepts no help or relief from anyone, even when it is urged upon him?
3. What progression do you see in this chapter in Nick's thoughts and attitudes toward the Woodsman?
4. Nick asks, "How could I be part of something so monstrous?" What do you think is the best answer to that question?
5. What was the chief cause of the Woodsman's death?

Chapter 11

1. How much is Nick to blame for the Woodsman dying?
2. What do you think the huge stone represents? The bloody heel of the woodsman and the crushed head of the beast?
3. Because of what has happened to the Woodsman, Nick detects that his journey "had been charted by an unseen hand, which had led me...to this moment." How well does that fit as a description of your own life's journey?

4. What does Nick have in common with the people the Woodsman is escorting across the tree? And what do you have in common with them?

5. Nick debates within himself if he really wants the Woodsman to come back for him. What is he struggling with?

Chapter 12

1. The Woodsman tells Nick, "The deed is done" and "The price is paid." What is the full meaning of this deed and this payment?

2. What does Nick's crossing equate to in your own life? Is this something you have already done? Is it something you need to do? Is it something you've been fearful of or avoiding for some other reason?

3. Why does Nick need to trust the Woodsman? And why is Nick hesitant to do this?

4. Why was it still impossible for Nick to cross the chasm on his own, even after the fallen tree had bridged it?

5. What are the biggest surprises for Nick in this chapter?

6. What seem to be the biggest questions still remaining in Nick's mind and heart?

7. What's most important for Nick to remember as he continues his journey toward Charis?

8. How do you think Nick can best explain to others what has happened to him?

To help you understand what the true "Woodsman" has done for you and how you can respond, find a Bible, and use the table of contents to help you locate the following passages. These are just a few of the passages in the Bible that can help you explore the truth about Jesus Christ; if you have questions as you read them, be sure to talk to a believer in Jesus to help you discover the answers.

- Isaiah—53:5–6 (if you're unfamiliar with a Bible, this means chapter 53 and verses 5 and 6 in that chapter)
- Mark—10:45 (words of Jesus)
- John—3:16–18 (words of Jesus)
- Romans—3:23–26; 5:6–11; 6:23; 10:9–13
- Ephesians—2:1–10
- 1 Peter—3:18
- 1 John—4:9–10; 5:11–13

After looking over these passages, ask yourself these questions:

- What are the most important truths about me in these passages?
- What are the most important truths about Jesus and what he has done for me?
- How do these passages tell me to respond to this truth? Have I done this?

The Woodsman tells Nick that he needs help understanding the book and the red road. Who do you have to help you deal with spiritual issues in your own life? How can you go about finding more help?

If you need assistance finding a Christ-centered, Bible-teaching church in your own area, contact the author's organization at info@epm.org.

About the Author

RANDY ALCORN is the founder and director of Eternal Perspective Ministries (EPM). Prior to EPM's beginning in 1990, he served as a pastor for fourteen years. He has spoken around the world and has taught on the adjunct faculties of Multnomah University and Western Seminary in Portland, Oregon.

Randy is the best-selling author of over thirty books with more than four million in print. He has written for many magazines and produces the popular periodical *Eternal Perspectives*. He's been a guest on over six hundred radio and television programs.

The father of two married daughters, Karina and Angela, Randy lives in Gresham, Oregon, with his wife and best friend, Nanci. They are the proud grandparents of four grandsons: Jake, Matt, Ty, and Jack. Randy enjoys hanging out with his family, biking, tennis, research, and reading.

You may contact Eternal Perspective Ministries by e-mail through their Web site at www.epm.org or at 39085 Pioneer Blvd., Suite 206, Sandy, OR 97055 or (503) 668-5200.

Follow Eternal Perspective Ministries on Facebook: www.facebook.com/EPMinistries and on their blog: www.epm.org/resources/.

Fiction from Randy Alcorn

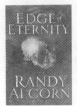

EDGE OF ETERNITY

A disillusioned business executive whose life has hit a dead-end confronts a profoundly clear view of his own past and personality, forcing him to finally consider the God he claims to believe does not exist.

THE ISHBANE CONSPIRACY

Four college students have worse troubles than midterms to contend with: A demonic contingent is after their souls.

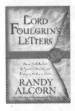

LORD FOULGRIN'S LETTERS

Lord Foulgrin's Letters invites believers to eavesdrop on their worst Enemy, learn his strategies and tricks, and discover how to ward off his devilish attacks.

DEADLINE • DOMINION • DECEPTION

Suspenseful fiction that offers a unique perspective on the search for meaning, the authority of truth, and the power of hope.

Printed in the United States
by Baker & Taylor Publisher Services